ERIE CANAL

ERIE CANAL

CANOEING AMERICA'S GREAT WATERWAY

PETER LOURIE

BOYDS MILLS PRESS

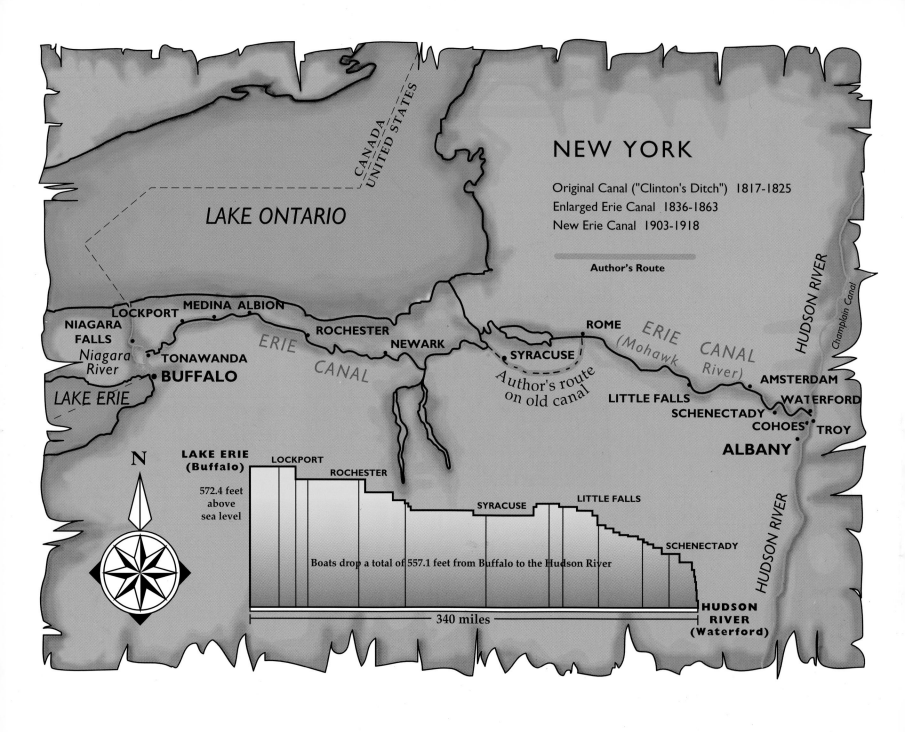

LAKE ONTARIO

CANADA
UNITED STATES

NEW YORK

Original Canal ("Clinton's Ditch") 1817-1825
Enlarged Erie Canal 1836-1863
New Erie Canal 1903-1918

Author's Route

NIAGARA
FALLS

LOCKPORT MEDINA ALBION

ROCHESTER

ROME

ERIE

HUDSON RIVER

Champlain Canal

*Niagara
River*

TONAWANDA

BUFFALO

ERIE

CANAL

NEWARK

SYRACUSE

Author's route
on old canal

(Mohawk

CANAL

River)

AMSTERDAM

WATERFORD

LITTLE FALLS

SCHENECTADY

COHOES

TROY

LAKE ERIE

ALBANY

N

**LAKE ERIE
(Buffalo)**

LOCKPORT

572.4 feet
above
sea level

ROCHESTER

SYRACUSE

LITTLE FALLS

HUDSON RIVER

SCHENECTADY

Boats drop a total of 557.1 feet from Buffalo to the Hudson River

340 miles

**HUDSON
RIVER
(Waterford)**

CONTENTS

PROLOGUE

After the Revolution, Americans yearned to settle the West. But reaching the "Promised Land" was a challenge. The early pioneers faced rugged mountains and dense forests, unnavigable rivers and dangerous waterfalls. They followed old Indian trails and trapper routes, and they blazed new trails of their own to reach the frontier.

To move settlers west and to bring the riches of the West back East, some even dreamed of joining the Atlantic Ocean with the Great Lakes by building an artificial river. They planned to dig a long ditch from the Hudson River all the way to Lake Erie! Many doubted it could be done. But the dreamers persisted. Because they did, the Erie Canal—or the "Big Ditch" as it was often called—became the first great technological achievement in the country's charge westward.

It took eight hard years of labor to build the Erie Canal. When it was finished, the Great Lakes had been yoked to the Atlantic Ocean by means of a forty-foot-wide and four-foot-deep channel of water.

The canal officially opened at ten o'clock on the morning of October 26, 1825. To mark the event, a cannon was fired in Buffalo, New York, on Lake Erie. Subsequent cannon fire relayed the message along the 363-mile canal to the Hudson River, then another 150 miles down the Hudson to New York City. Before the age of telephones, the cannon fire message had traveled more than 1000 miles, all the way to the Atlantic Ocean and back to Buffalo in only three hours and twenty minutes.

Almost two hundred years later, the Erie Canal is still in operation. In order to see what the canal looks like today, I decided to paddle its entire distance by canoe. The small boat would allow me to travel as slowly as the first canallers. Paddling east I would follow the same route of the canal boats that once brought the timber, produce, and freight out of the West to help build the great cities of the East.

Part of my plan was to paddle my way home. Traveling on the Erie Canal and on other waterways, I realized I would be able to paddle to within a mile of my house in Vermont—from Lake Erie!

I wanted to travel the Erie like the canallers of old.
(circa 1890)

PART I

THE WESTERN CANAL

CREATION OF THE CANAL

My family and I packed the car with my gear, and we drove to Lake Erie in downtown Buffalo. From the historic terminus of the Erie Canal, I launched my canoe and waved good-bye. I felt sad that I wouldn't see my family for three weeks, but I was excited about taking a long trip alone in a canoe.

Under a bright gray sky I paddled away from the city, north along the shore of the lake. Empty grain elevators hundreds of feet high reminded me of Buffalo's former glory in the wheat trade. I quickly entered the Niagara River, which joins Lake Erie to Lake Ontario, and passed underneath two bridges connecting the United States to Canada.

For the first fifteen miles of my trip on the Niagara River,

De Witt Clinton

I followed U.S. Interstate 190. The busy highway runs directly over the old canal, which used to run parallel to the river. The original Erie Canal has been filled in here and covered with pavement.

There is a good reason why the old canallers did not want to use the Niagara River. It was a lot easier to travel on the still water in a canal. Before the steam-powered tugs, mules alone could not pull heavy canal boats through the twelve-mile-an-hour river current.

At least a hundred years before the Erie Canal was actually built, Americans had thought about building a great shipping canal to reach the interior. In 1772, Benjamin Franklin wrote, "Rivers are ungovernable things, especially in hilly countries. Canals are quiet and very manageable." George Washington, who had trained as a surveyor, understood that rivers and a series of canals would be the best way to connect the western wilderness with the eastern cities.

The vision for the Grand Western Canal, as the Erie was called, was made real by De Witt Clinton, the governor of the state of New York. Clinton made it his mission to build a 363-mile canal through the wilderness to join Lake Erie with the Hudson River.

With no help from the federal government, Clinton raised enough money to begin construction of the canal, spearheading the biggest engineering job yet attempted in America. Before picks and shovels broke the ground, the Erie engineers studied the canals of Europe. One engineer,

Entering the canal from the Niagara River.

Canvass White, walked 2,000 miles along the canals of England, taking notes and making drawings.

The present-day Erie Canal begins in the city of Tonawanda, north of Buffalo. Here, a few miles before reaching Niagara Falls, I found the narrow channel that shoots eastward away from the river. I also met hurricane Fran in Tonawanda. She had been pounding the East Coast for days, and was kicking up the river, blowing a bitter wind in my face. My arms began to cramp. I stopped to rest, but the wind drove my canoe backward. Fortunately I spotted the canal and turned east into the wind. Coming off the wide Niagara

River and into the narrow canal was a relief. The canal has a gentle current.

I paddled in the drizzling rain until my arms grew numb. Only twenty-two days to go! The rainfly on my canoe, a canvas cover made especially for this trip, had kept most of my gear dry. I was soaked and exhausted when finally I found a place to camp. Bad weather is a large part of canal folklore, even if some of the songs were sung in jest:

> *We were forty miles from Albany*
> *Forget it I never shall;*
> *What a terrible storm we had that night*
> *On the E-ri-e Canal.*

The actual digging of the Erie Canal, the longest canal in the United States, began toward the center of the proposed canal on July 4, 1817, in Rome, New York. Thousands of workers used picks, shovels, spades, buckets, wheelbarrows, scrapers, and plows. Tools were invented for the digging. A huge stump puller and tree cutter were devised to speed the construction. In five months, fifteen miles of the canal were completed. It would take another eight years to finish the project. Engineering problems lay ahead.

One song about building the canal went like this:

> *We are digging the Ditch through the mire;*
> *Through the mud and slime and the mire, by heck!*

From construction to enlargements and repairs, work never ceased on the canal. (circa 1898)

And the mud is our principal hire;
Up our pants, in our shirts, down our neck, by heck!
We are digging the Ditch through the gravel,
So the people and freight can travel!

THE CANAL'S ACHIEVEMENT

When the canal finally opened in October, 1825, Governor Clinton boarded a packet boat called the *Seneca Chief* and led an armada of boats from Buffalo to Albany. The trip from Lake Erie to Albany took only seven days. Before the construction of the canal, the trip would have taken more than a

A packet boat in the "Deep Cut." (circa 1825)

Locks 34 & 35 at Lockport.

month by land. Packet boats were the long narrow "stage-coaches" of the canal. They carried up to a hundred passengers at about four miles an hour—the same speed I can paddle my canoe. When the *Seneca Chief* reached Albany, it traveled another three days down the Hudson River to New York City. In a ceremony known as the "Wedding of the Waters," Governor Clinton poured Lake Erie water from kegs into the Atlantic Ocean. The dream had come true. The East and the West had been joined.

The first two locks on the Erie today are at Lockport. There are thirty-four locks on the canal, and I would pass through them all. Locks, water chambers with gates at each end, are needed to raise and lower boats from one water level to another. Lake Erie is 572 feet above sea level, and in order to reach the Hudson River at Waterford, boats must drop a total of 557 feet.

A geological ridge called the Niagara Escarpment runs along the top of New York State from Niagara Falls through Lockport to Rochester. This rock ledge presented an engineering nightmare for the canal builders. The escarpment was blasted with dynamite. Tons of blasted rock were hauled out by cranes moving high overhead. It was a dangerous job. One thousand workers took three years to make a deep cut through seven miles of rock. When it was completed, a trench twenty-seven feet wide and up to thirty feet deep had been cut through the escarpment. Then a towpath was chiseled into the rock face for the mules.

In the lock.

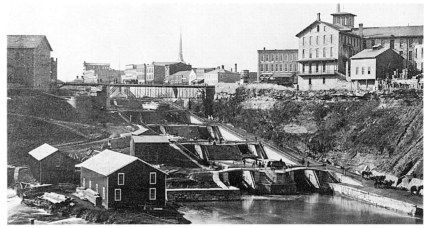

An old flight of locks at Lockport today.

To get boats up and down the sixty-foot-high escarpment, the engineers originally built two sets of five small locks, each with a drop of twelve feet. These small locks were replaced in 1918 by two larger locks.

I paddled into the first of these locks, Lock 35, which has a drop of 24.5 feet. The gates on the upstream side of the lock point in a V, so the water pressure keeps them closed. As the lock operator closed the gates behind me, I could hear the grinding of valves opening to let the water out downstream. The Erie locks do not use pumps to fill or drain the lock chambers. Water is moved in and out of the chamber by gravity. The water doesn't drop fast enough to make your stomach rise into your throat, but three million gallons running out of a 300-foot concrete tub is a lot of water. And my canoe was the only boat in the chamber!

As the water rushed out the other side of the lock, the canoe dropped slowly but steadily on the swirling surface.

17

I felt very small in this huge chamber.

And on to the next lock.

Nearly twenty-five feet below the top, in a dungeon of darkness, I looked up to see the lock operator standing on the edge of the lock wall. When the water level in the chamber reached its lowest level, the gates opened and I paddled into Lock 34, where the procedure was repeated for another drop that was 24.6 feet. The whole operation took about an hour.

After Lockport, a long stretch of the western canal has no locks. Here the artificial river runs through beautiful farmland where willows line the banks. Hazy sunshine followed my first few days of rain, and a gentle wind carried the peaceful chirping of crickets. The canal bed has been built up here, and I rode high above the landscape at the level of the treetops and the roofs of houses.

I passed old stone quarries near Medina, which are no longer mined. I saw only a few boats each day, none of them tugs or barges. Looking at the quiet canal, it's hard to imagine how busy the Erie must have been in the early 1800s. If I were paddling the canal 150 years ago, I might have seen a boat pass by every few minutes.

By 1835 a thousand settlers a day stepped off the canal boats at the western terminus in Buffalo and boarded lake steamers for the trip westward on the Great Lakes. The population of Ohio, Indiana, Illinois, and Michigan exploded from less than 800,000 in 1820 to over 4 million by 1850.

In 1845, an estimated 4,000 boats worked the Erie with 25,000 men, women, and children. Five thousand were boy mule drivers, often as young as thirteen and fourteen years old. Boats lined up all the way across the state like two columns of ants—the one heading west often carrying people; the other heading east usually bearing freight. Along the elevated towpath, mules and horses pulled a variety of boats—packets, line boats, lakers, bullheads, deck scows, icebreakers, gospel boats, library boats, and even circus boats with wild animals in cages.

Traffic jams at the crowded locks led to fights over which boat would go through first. Rooming houses, grocery stores, taverns, and industries lined the banks of the bustling canal. Ten years after it was completed, the canal, called "Clinton's Ditch" by those who doubted its success, had earned back its entire investment through tolls.

The Erie Canal became so busy that it was expanded twice. The original canal, only forty feet wide and four feet deep, was enlarged to handle the growing number of boats. Completed in 1863, this new version of the canal, often called the First Enlargement, was seventy feet wide and seven feet deep. This too was abandoned when steam-powered boats became more prevalent in the early 1900s, and the canal was rebuilt a second and final time.

From 1903 to 1918, the Erie was enlarged to its present size, as much as 200 feet wide and 12 feet deep. This most recent phase of the Erie Canal is part of the New York State Barge Canal System, which includes smaller canals such as the sixty-mile Champlain Canal that runs from Troy to Lake Champlain.

The canal was a busy place at the turn of the century.

A lift bridge on the western canal.

For every windy and wave-battering day on a canoe trip, a day of good weather comes along. That's a lesson I've learned from a lifetime exploring rivers, and it held true for the Erie Canal.

My trip began in rain and headwinds. A few days later, the wind turned around out of the west, and I paddled perhaps five miles an hour with the wind shoving me from behind. I shouted for joy when the sun came out. Only 400 miles to paddle until I reached home!

I passed under many lift bridges on the western portion of the canal. The equipment that raises some of the older bridges in towns such as Medina, Albion, and Brockport dates from the early part of the century. The bridges on the original canal, however, didn't go up and down. To save construction costs, the 300 stationary bridges that spanned the Big Ditch were built only seven and a half feet above the

"Low bridge! Everybody down!"
(circa 1852)

water. The famous song *Low Bridge, Everybody Down* records the warning to passengers to duck as they passed under the bridges:

> *I got a mule, her name is Sal,*
> *Fifteen miles on the Erie Canal!*
> *She's a good old worker and good old pal*
> *Fifteen miles on the Erie Canal!*
> *We've hauled some barges in our day,*
> *Filled with lumber, coal, and hay*
> *And we know ev'ry inch of the way*
> *from Albany to Buffalo*
> *Low bridge, ev'rybody down,*
> *Low bridge 'cause we're coming to a town…*

PART 2

THE CENTRAL CANAL

A ROUGH-AND-TUMBLE WORLD

I found old canal ruins not fifty yards from the Newark lock. Buried deep in earth and grass, massive blocks of stone peeked out of the past like ancient Roman foundations. These limestone blocks dated from the 1840s when the canal was first enlarged. If these stones could speak, they would tell countless stories. Standing there I wished they could have told me tales of the laborers who had built the canal. Many were Irish, who fled mass starvation in their own country and found work in America building the Erie. An eyewitness described how these men worked "knee deep in the wet muck" wearing flannel shirts and slouch caps.

I imagined what life might have been like for the Irish immigrants and also for the thousands of Eastern Europeans and Italians who came to build the second enlargement early in this century. The songs they left behind give us a clue:

> *A life on the raging canawl,*
> *A home on its muddy deep,*
> *Where through summer, spring, and fall,*
> *The frogs their vigil keep.*
> *Like a fish on the hook I pine,*
> *On this dull unchanging shore—*
> *Oh give me the packet line,*
>   *And the muddy canawl's dull roar.*

The canaller's life was a rugged one, and the canal could be a dangerous place. That rough-and-tumble world is gone now, living only in legends and folk songs.

Each day I passed a few more cabin cruisers and sailboats with their masts lying on the deck so they could get under the bridges. I'm sure the old canallers would have been amazed at the sight of these pleasure boats heading south to Florida or the Caribbean for the winter.

The sun had disappeared into clouds, and the rain had returned. Fortunately, I met a friendly couple who offered me a ride on their boat. I was tired and wet, so I jumped aboard with my canoe and rode for twenty miles in the gray drizzle.

When I paddled into the lock at Lyons, I was excited because I knew it wouldn't be long before I would pass by the remaining arches of the Richmond aqueduct that once took

Ruins of an old lock in Newark.

FACING PAGE: ***Remains of the Richmond aqueduct.***

The Richmond aqueduct. (circa 1905)

Here's how an aqueduct carried the canal over the Mohawk River. Note the mule team far in advance of the boat. (circa 1900)

FACING PAGE: *Hard work and sickness went hand in hand. (circa 1872)*

boats over the Seneca River in the Montezuma Swamp. It was built by a man named Van Rensselaer Richmond. I was looking forward to seeing this relic, because most of the aqueducts that once carried the canal over rivers, streams, and valleys are gone.

The mule- and horse-pulled canal boats that ran on the original and enlarged Erie Canal had no motors to fight a river's current. Rivers might flood in the spring or dry up in the summer. In order for the canal to bypass the undependable rivers, magnificent stone aqueducts with great Roman arches were built to carry the boats, the mules, and the people, high over the water.

HUMAN COST

In one canal town, I found a hill once called Cholera Hill, where the bodies of dead canal workers are buried in unmarked graves. Disease was common in the communities along the canal. The most dangerous was cholera.

Epidemics of cholera, also known as "the destroyer," swept along the canal at different times. Few towns were spared. During an epidemic some canallers fled to higher terrain. Stores and businesses closed. Canal boats stopped running. It was little known at the time that cholera infection occurs from drinking contaminated water. Many believed that tar smoke could clear the air of the destroyer. Great billows of smelly black smoke rose into the sky above the canal,

26

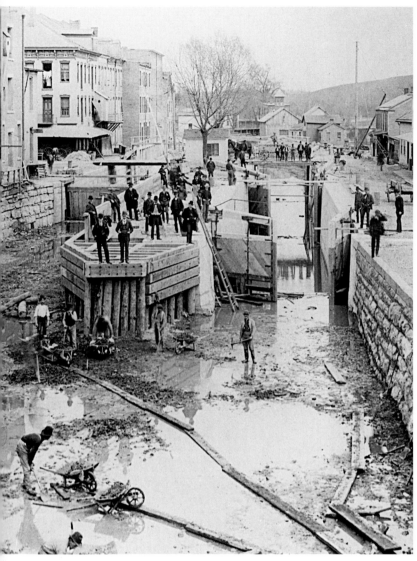

The men worked under difficult conditions. (circa 1885)
FACING PAGE: *The Erie House. Peter Van Detto is the man with the dog. (circa 1900)*

which acted as a highway for the disease. Infected passengers who had traveled the canal boarded lake steamers and traveled west, carrying the disease with them. They traveled down the Mississippi and the Ohio rivers, spreading the deadly cholera to settlers and Native Americans as far away as Fort Union on the Upper Missouri River.

At Lock 25 I met a canaller named Steve Wunder. He asked me if I would like to see the Erie House, an early nineteenth-century tavern in Port Byron, one of the forgotten towns along a former version of the Erie.

Legends and ghost stories abound along the canal. The Erie House is one of them. In the dark of night I stood in front of the tavern, built on the bank of the abandoned enlarged canal, now a mere depression in the earth. Steve took me inside.

A man named Peter Van Detto had operated the tavern and rooming house for decades. His two daughters had died only a few years ago. They had lived in the Erie House all their lives and kept it looking just as it had for decades. Now Steve was turning the Erie House into a museum.

We entered the old house, and Steve led the way to the guest rooms upstairs. The wood creaked under our feet. We tried the lights, but they weren't working. Moving in the dark, we bumped into beds and chairs.

When we reached the back room, Steve said in a deep and scary voice, "This was Annie's room." Annie, I learned, was a cook on a canal boat who boarded in the Erie House

around the turn of the century. People say she was a beautiful woman with flaming red hair. One day Annie mysteriously disappeared. Newspapers reported that she was last seen at the Erie House. Legend has it that Peter Van Detto was in love with her. Some people suspected she was murdered by his jealous wife. Annie's disappearance remains a mystery to this day.

The room was dark, but my eyes adjusted until I could see silhouettes of what might have been Annie's furniture, a simple bed and chair. Some say that Annie still walks the rooms of the Erie House. One night Steve's wife believed she saw a shadowy figure at Annie's window. Could it have been the ghost of Annie herself?

After my visit with "Annie," Steve wished me good luck on my journey. I slept only a few hours, then I started out in the dark rain at five in the morning.

The feel of the canal changes in the central section. The dense, dripping foliage looks like something out of the bayous of Mississippi. Birds of all kinds flock through the tendrils, including eagles. I watched kingfishers diving at the water like fireworks. Blue herons squawked when I interrupted their fishing. I paddled up to them so quietly they exploded in angry surprise.

In 1818 the soggy ground of the Montezuma Swamp made canal digging difficult. Here the men waited until winter when the ground froze and digging would be easier.

I found no dry place to camp, so I pushed onward to

Syracuse for the night. I paddled more than thirty miles against the waves and ate chocolate, peanuts, and raisins for energy. I drank lots and lots of water.

DAILY LIFE ON THE CANAL

Thirty miles of the enlarged 1850s canal, a section from Syracuse to Rome, still has water enough for paddling a canoe, but it's much too shallow for motors and big boats. To reach this section, I would have to make a seven-mile portage through downtown Syracuse. I walked my canoe on Erie Boulevard, passing the old Weighlock Building, which is now the Erie Canal Museum. Early on Sunday morning a few people caught the odd sight of a man carrying a canoe over the old canal, now filled in and covered with pavement.

The original 1825 canal and the enlarged canal have been paved over in the downtown section of cities such as Syracuse. In Buffalo, Rochester, Rome, Utica, Schenectady, and Albany, the only evidence of the old canal route is the name of the streets where the canal once flowed—Erie Boulevard, Canal Street, and Erie Street.

In order to pay for the millions of dollars it cost to build the canal, tolls were charged by New York State. The Syracuse Weighlock Building was one of few places on the canal where the boats were weighed. Tolls were collected based on the weight of the boat's cargo.

The old Weighlock Building, now the Erie Canal Museum in Syracuse: I'm walking where the canal used to flow.

The Weighlock Building. (circa 1905)

Syracuse in 1907 after the collapse of the Onondaga Creek aqueduct on the Erie Canal. (circa 1907)

A train rumbles overhead as a canoeist in front of me reaches a low bridge.

The horses or mules pulled the boat into the lock chamber inside the Weighlock Building. The weighmaster drained the water from the chamber, and the boat came to rest on a platform attached to a scale. After the boat had been weighed and the tolls calculated, the chamber was filled, and the boat continued onward. The procedure took approximately fifteen minutes.

Over time the railroads competed with the canal. In order to keep customers shipping cargo by canal instead of by rail, tolls were abolished in 1883. These tolls had been an extremely successful way to pay for the canal's construction. By 1883, 121 million dollars had been collected.

East of Syracuse, in Dewitt, I crossed over Butternut Creek on a tiny aqueduct. Finally I was canoeing the old canal. I saw not a single boat the entire day. Here the canal is only seventy feet wide. Remnants of old boats were half sunk into the sand bars. I had to maneuver through downed trees and under low bridges crisscrossed with spider webs. The canal had grown so shallow, my paddle touched bottom. Five-pound carp lazily fed on the surface and splashed me when I surprised them.

Wild apple and pear trees grow all along the abandoned canal. I could just imagine how a hundred years ago children might have thrown their apple pits from passing boats onto shore, where the trees took root. Perhaps the boys leading their mules picked fruit as they passed slowly by, maybe their only meal for the day.

A small aqueduct carried me over Butternut Creek.

34

Some children lived on boats with their animals.
(circa 1852)

Generations of children grew up on the Erie Canal. Families ate, slept, and played aboard their canal boats. The children had little privacy. Moving constantly from town to town, they lacked neighborhood friends. When the canal closed for the winter, they went to school from December to March. Then the Erie would open up again, and the children would leave school for the canal. After they turned twelve, the children drove the mules along the towpath. Mothers would tie ropes around the younger children for safety. When they fell off the boat, they were hauled back on deck.

The quiet beauty of the old canal made me aware of the fast pace of my life at home. Here on the old Erie, I was learning how to slow down, enjoy the sights and sounds of nature, and focus on one thing alone—paddling paddling paddling. Most days I canoed for eight to ten hours, and traveled from twenty to thirty miles. For my first night on the old canal, however, I decided to camp after only ten miles. I wanted this pastoral journey to last a little longer.

Camping on the canal.

When they turned twelve, boys
worked the mule teams. (circa 1900)

Some boats carried their own mule teams. (circa 1905)

It was a lonely job walking far ahead of the boat. (circa 1900)

In Rome I visited the Erie Canal Village, where the canal was started on July 4, 1817. Here I met a man who drove mules for a tourist boat. He told me that mule drivers were called *hoggees,* presumably from a Scottish word for laborer. A hoggee was often a young boy who worked two six-hour shifts, rain or shine. Walking miles along the towpath, he was not allowed to ride the mules. The night shifts could be lonely. The tow-rope to the boat was at least 200 feet long. During the graveyard shift, it must have been spooky to walk along the towpath alone so far ahead of the boat. Some boats carried their own mule teams in a stable in the bow. Others, like the swifter packet boats with passengers aboard and no room for housing animals, required fresh teams from stables along the canal.

Outside of Rome, I returned to the much wider new Erie Canal, where I became a paddling machine with only one thought in mind—home!

PART 3

THE EASTERN CANAL

USING RIVERS AND LAKES

The eastern part of the Erie Canal is no longer a ditch filled with water, but rather a river that has been dredged for tugs and barges. Of the many lakes and rivers used by the new Erie Canal, the Mohawk River is the most important. The Mohawk, flowing from Rome all the way to the Hudson, was a water highway for Native Americans for thousands of years before the Europeans arrived. A hundred years before the canal was built, the Mohawk was traveled by settlers heading west.

The Mohawk formed the only gap in the Appalachian Plateau, a mountain chain stretching from the St. Lawrence Valley in the north to Georgia in the south. This river corridor, this break in the mountains, was the reason a canal in

A lock at Little Falls. (circa 1890)

The gate looked like a great guillotine.

New York State was first envisioned as a possible waterway to the West. Today the Mohawk River, the New York State Thruway, and Conrail all run close to one another through the mountain gap. Until perhaps twenty years ago, a canoeist in this section might have spotted a lot of commercial traffic. Today I saw not a single tugboat. Islands and coves appeared as the river spread out. As the terrain grew hilly, I passed through narrow corridors of rock.

In one of these rocky corridors, the canal runs through a beautiful old town called Little Falls. These little falls are more like a set of rapids that run wild in the spring. Before the canal was built, river traffic had to get around them. Flat-bottomed cargo boats called *bateaux* were portaged until, in 1790, a small canal was built to route boats around the falls. I saw the crumbling remains of the aqueduct that once brought the boats over the river. Nearby factories were boarded shut. These sights were silent reminders of the Erie Canal's boom years.

Lock 17 at Little Falls has one of the highest lift locks of its type in the world, dropping 40.5 feet. It holds five million gallons of water, and I shared this cavern of steel and concrete with three high-tech cabin cruisers. The water swirled as it left the chamber, and the lift gate, which looks like a massive guillotine, rose slowly, dripping a torrent of water. I paddled like crazy to get under it, fearing it might fall and chop me in half.

The Erie Canal faced competition from the railroad.
(circa 1890)

Passing through Amsterdam.

Even after weeks of paddling, my arms were stiff every morning, but the pain faded by noon. Paddling can become tedious. Some days it helped to chant or hum—and think about my family. I was getting closer to home each day.

Late in the afternoon I reached Amsterdam, the "Rug City." Formerly known for its thriving carpet mills, Amsterdam's smokestacks no longer smoke. Factories have been boarded up or have burned to the ground.

Freight and passenger trains rattled past me every half hour on the north shore of the Mohawk. Trucks and cars on U.S. Interstate 90 whined constantly on the south shore. Up above I saw jet trails streaking the sky. I felt like the tortoise compared to the hare in my slow-moving canoe. Now I had a dramatic sense of why the great days of the Erie Canal had come to an end. The "Big Ditch" could not compete with the breakneck speed of modern transportation. In some ways, the Erie's days were numbered from the start.

When the canal first opened in 1825, other visionaries were already talking about building railroads. A few years after the "Ditch" was finished, a direct rail line was completed between Lake Erie and Albany. In 1849, four trains a day left Albany for Buffalo. The fastest of these could take passengers the whole route in a mere fifteen hours. By the 1850s most passengers rode New York Central trains west while some freight still went by canal. The trains, and later the trucks

The site of the entrance to the Erie Canal from the Hudson River. (circa 1825)

The same site—but times have changed.

and the planes, eventually stole most of the canal's commerce.

The first day of autumn dawned sunny and cool. It would be my last day of paddling the Erie Canal. The strong westerly wind was at my back.

A friend from Vermont named John Housekeeper joined me for my final day on the Erie. He paddled in a sea kayak. After the General Electric plant in Schenectady, we passed a huge landfill on the backside of the city of Cohoes. It smelled horrible, and we wondered if polluted waste was seeping from the dump into the canal. From here, John and I could see the first lock of five that would take us down to the Hudson River.

Former versions of the canal went south through the textile-manufacturing town of Cohoes. But today the new Erie takes a more direct easterly route to the Hudson.

I once drove through Cohoes to see the abandoned locks of the old canal. Then I drove five more miles to Albany, capital of New York, to Erie Street, the very place where the first Erie Canal lock had taken boats off the Hudson in the 1800s.

Today the historic eastern terminus of the canal is paved. Everything has changed, just as it has on the other end of the canal, where I had begun my canoe journey weeks ago.

John and I reached the final set of locks late in the afternoon. This flight of five locks takes two and a half hours to drop 169 feet to the level of the Hudson. Each lock has a

Coming to the final set of locks.

Meredith "Blondie" Connor

Blondie spent a lifetime on tugs like this one. (circa 1938)

drop of at least 30 feet. It was easy paddling after all the hard work crossing the state.

Canada geese flew south over our heads. The autumn sun slanted orange off the brick mills.

I heard a far-off whistle, which made me think about trains. I thought how one technology replaces another. Mule-pulled canal boats went out of business when the tugs started to pull barges in the late 1800s. Then even tugs and barges began to disappear in the latter part of this century when the trains, trucks, and airplanes could haul more freight in less time.

I met one old tug captain named "Blondie." He had worked his whole life on tugs through the canal and on the Great Lakes. He sat on his porch and spoke of days gone by. "Everything is different now," he said. When he began to recall a lifetime on the busy canal, he looked far off into the distance, a little sad I thought. But he said he was happy to be home after so many years of travel. Now he could rest and remember.

When the metal doors opened on the last lock, we paddled out past Waterford. Here at last was the Hudson River, gateway to the Atlantic. From here I could paddle down to New York City. Or I could travel north to my home in Vermont. Each was about 150 miles away.

Of course I chose home.

EPILOGUE

HOME

For the next seven days I paddled hard, first against the wind and the Hudson River current, then up the Champlain Canal into Lake Champlain, which forms the border between New York and Vermont. When I reached the wide lake, the wind was at my back. The waves were so big they nearly knocked me over.

The lake is a paradise for birds. I saw cormorants, snow geese, gulls, and terns. I camped at Mt. Independence across from Fort Ticonderoga, where Benedict Arnold had stopped the oncoming British fleet in 1776. Thousands of soldiers had died here in the winter of 1777 from disease and starvation.

The night was winter-dark, except for the full moon, and

the temperature dropped well below freezing. For the last time until the year 2000, the moon went dark in a full lunar eclipse. I missed it, though, for I was fast asleep in my tent.

On my last day I paddled up Otter Creek. The wind gusted to fifty miles per hour. Sometimes my canoe stood still in the water, even though I kept paddling.

In midafternoon, the sky brightened, and I saw a happy sight—my family waiting for me on the banks of Otter Creek. I could hardly believe I hadn't seen them in three weeks.

While the great days of the Erie Canal have already passed into history, the canal is on the threshold of a new era. More and more people realize that the Erie is a living museum, a place where the Industrial Revolution generated goods for the growing nation, an artery that allowed the nation's lifeblood to flow. Signs of revitalization are cropping up in towns all along the canal. This ribbon of water that crosses the Empire State is more than a remnant of past glory. It is a symbol of America—the first step in a technological march that led to trains, to airplanes, to spaceships, and . . . to what next?

I was happy to be home. But I was equally glad that I'd traveled hundreds of miles on one of the great waterways of America—the artificial river that had opened the West. Out of the country's heartland, I'd followed a water trail to the people I love most. Home, I realized, is indeed connected by water to the world and to the history of our nation.

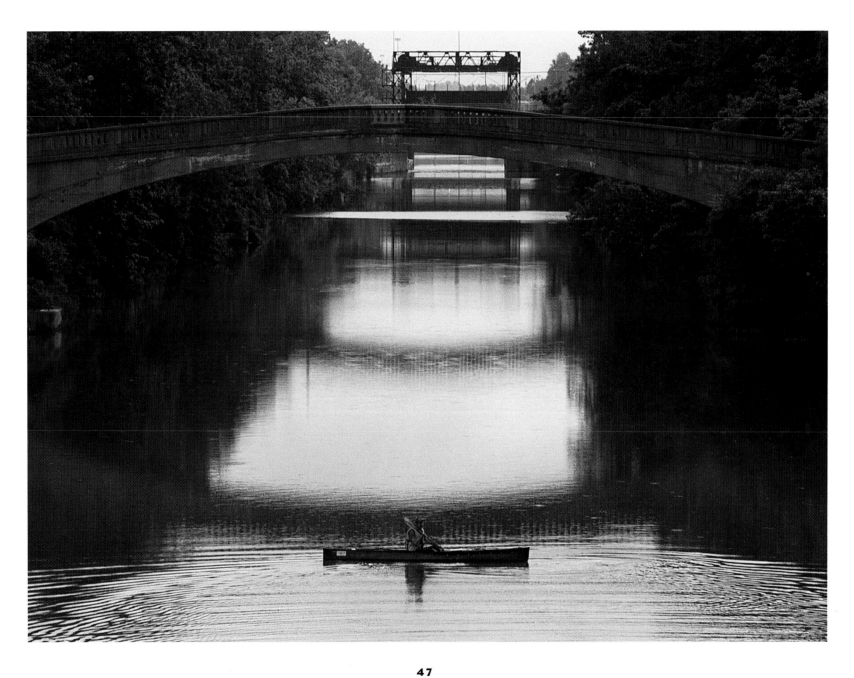

To learn more about rivers, contact RiverResource, an educational resource on the
World Wide Web devoted to the rivers of the world
http://www.highlands.com/RiverResource

Special thanks to Craig Williams and Tom Grasso

Text and photographs copyright © 1997 by Peter Lourie
Additional photographs: Lisa Pierce: pp. 7, 10, 13, top left 17 & 18
Jim Shaughnessy: pp. 42, 43; Steve Gurney: pp. 38, 40, 41; James Patrick Haley p. 47
New York State Museum: p. 12
Canal Society of New York State: pp. 5, 6, 9, 15, 16, 17, 19, 21, 23, 26, 27, 28, 29, 31,
32, 34, 35, 36, 37, 40, 41, 42, 43, & back jacket
Map illustration on page 4 by Gordon Tin

Published by Caroline House
Boyds Mills Press, Inc.
A Highlights Company
815 Church Street
Honesdale, Pennsylvania 18431
Printed in China

Publisher Cataloging-in-Publication Data

Lourie, Peter.
   Erie Canal : canoeing America's great waterway / by Peter
Lourie.—1st ed.
[48]p. : col.ill. ; cm.
Summary : An informative essay about a trip across the Erie Canal, complemented by
photographs.
ISBN 1-56397-764-8
1. Erie Canal (N.Y.)—Children's literature. [1. Erie Canal (N.Y.).]
I. Title.
974.7—dc20   1997   AC   CIP
Library of Congress Catalog Card Number 96-80393

First Boyds Mills Press paperback edition, 1999
Book designed by Abby Kagan/King Kong Cody Design
The text of this book is set in 13/17pt Goudy

10 9 8 7 6 5 4 3 2